ALSO BY SARAH GARLAND

Coming to Tea
Going Shopping
Having a Picnic
Polly's Puffin

For Cobbett

British Library Cataloguing
in Publication Data
Garland, Sarah
Doing the washing.
I. Title
823′.914 [J] PZ7
ISBN 0−370−30948−0

Printed and bound in Italy for
The Bodley Head Ltd
32 Bedford Square, London WC1B 3SG
by L.E.G.O., Vicenza, Italy
First published 1983
Reprinted 1985, 1989

DOING THE WASHING
Sarah Garland

THE BODLEY HEAD
London

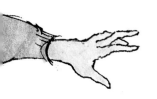

Time for all the dirty clothes

to go into the washing machine.

Soap in. Switch on.

The clothes go round and round.
Water gushes out...

until at last all the
clothes are clean.

Down the stairs we go.

Hang up the socks.

Hang up the pants.

Hang up the vests.

Down the garden to hang
up the sheets.

The washing's done.
Time for a drink.

Time for a story.